Momma said, Momma said

By T.L. Hawkins

Forward

I am abundantly honored to put pen to paper and present my sister, Tracy Hawkins' literary work, Momma Said Momma Said.

Momma Said Momma Said started out as a book of wisdom, wit, laughter and advice that celebrates the life of me and the author's dearly beloved Mother who left behind boundless wisdom, wit and lessons on life. However, the author embedded with her own innate wisdom, felt it best to celebrate the wisdom, wits and quotes of Mother's both with us and the ones who have made their transition to the other side. Mothers are near and dear to the hearts of everyone who are familiar with the unselfish and unconditional love of a grandmother, Mother, aunt, sister, friend, confidant, spiritual advisor, BFF and the like.

Momma Said Momma Said is a must read. When reading it, you are sure to reflect on and become mindful of the advice given by your own beloved Mother? You are sure to recall and reflect on the advice given and wasn't heeded only to discover that the advice given takes up a warm and special place in your heart.

Momma Said Momma Said is a brief story best appreciated with a group of special girlfriends on a retreat, a good read to pick up after a long day at the office, or a book that will feed you in that moment you long to reach out and enjoy the warm embrace of a Mother's love.

While reading you might experience moments of joy, sadness, laughter, tears, rejuvenation and elation. You will not be alone. Your Momma Said, Momma Said friends across the globe share in your joy, sadness, laughter and tears as you relish in the reflection of the wisdom, life and knowledge left behind by Mothers. Momma Said Momma Said is a must read by all who are keenly are of the unselfish love and wisdom Mothers embodies,

Wanda Hawkins,

Ordained Pastor, Counselor and Spiritual advisor

Introduction

How significant is my life?

Do I make a difference?

When I move, when I act, when I do something, does the universe notice?

This book is a testimony for every Mother clenching a dream for her children. There are words of advice and wisdom that Mothers have been sharing with their children since the beginning of time. Don't be surprised if the collection that follows remind you of something your Momma said.

This is a challenge for women to remember playing the childhood game called house. Remember playing that game for hours upon hours and reenacting the roles of family members that swirled around in our lives. Remember everyone wanted the coveted role of Mother. We really took the role of make believe Momma serious. If you were going to be Momma you had to come correct.

After all the bickering, pushing and outright name calling it was agreed the girl with the most endearing traits should be Momma. You had to be stern, know how to cook, have a heart big as the ocean, loving smile, embracing arms; if you possessed those qualities, the role was yours.

Let's face it, if the role of Momma is played correctly in real or make believe, we put our Mothers on a pedestal. The respect is most definitely there, but what we really feel is simple awe and admiration. Even as little girls we knew it took a special person to be a mom. Ok, mom is some kind of special, she bore you in this world even though she had the choice not to. Yea, even back in the day the choice was up to the woman whether she would bear a child or not.

Now it took an even better person to be a good Mother, she was a cut above the rest. This woman would forsake everything for the good of her children. All of her dreams and hopes for herself are put on hold so her offspring could realize theirs. This Mother would forgo basic necessities so that her children would not be without. I'm talking about never fixing a dinner plate and always eating what the children didn't eat. Even if the children ate everything, the Mother ate nothing. She would wear the same ratty house dress so her children had decent clothes to keep other children from make fun of them. This Mother always had time for her children, even after working two jobs for very little pay. If her children feel down, this Mother was always there to lift the children's sprit, even though many times it was her sprits that needed the lifting.

So Mothers as we watch our children play that timeless game house, let us hope that we can be half the Mother to them that our Mother was to us.

Now, the black Mother is all that and a bag of chips because she had to be strong. The black Mother was a deep well of spiritual strength that comes from simply being. Hazel used to always say, "Chile, I didn't always know how I was gonna feed y'all, but prayer helps, and in the sunlight breakfast was served."

Momma was a renaissance woman.

More than 70 years ago when my mother left Little Rock Arkansas she knew there was something more than picking bales and bales of cotton for a mere $.20 a season. Yep that's what she got paid .20 for the summer and spring.

I remember asking momma why she picked the cotton. Oh, the ignorance of youth, but momma didn't scorn me; her answer was text book Hazel Lee Garrett, "I bowed my back so that my children wouldn't have to." Talk about humbling.

When I think of the great woman who was my mom, I often reflect back to the words of another great woman. "I have plowed and planted and gathered into barns and no man could head me...And ain't I a woman? I could work as much and eat as much as a man — when I could get to it — and bear the lash as well and ain't I a woman? I have born 13 children and seen most all sold into slavery and when I cried out a Mother's grief none but Jesus heard me... And ain't I a woman?"

Sojourner Truth

Hazel lee Garrett felt the south was oppressive. She had dreams of a world that had nothing to do with picking cotton from sun up to sun down. In 1940, she made a bold move and called up her Aunt Frankie and asked if she could move to Chicago with her. She assured Aunt Frankie she was use to hard work, but she wanted to do it on her terms.

So her journey began. She joined the thousands of people that made the big migration north and she never looked back. Momma often said, "Regrets were a waste of time."

She vowed that nothing would stop her from making something of herself. Truth be told, Momma wanted to become a nurse. She had a nurturing nature that was her calling.

As it is with many journeys and many dreams, one is inclined to encounter detours that force one to reexamine the future. Such was the case with Momma when she encountered her husband Artilus Hawkins.

Mommas and her husband soon parted ways forcing Momma to put her old dreams away and focus on my big Brother, her firstborn child Artilus Hawkins and thus began the real journey. Momma went on to have nine more children, Gregory, Orlando, Anthony and Phyllis (twins) Wanda, Terry and Tyrone, (twins) Yolanda and Tracy (me).

Following are words of wisdom from Hazel and other Mothers used to get all of their children through this journey called life.

Nothing comes to a sleeper but a dream...

I lead with this simple statement told to all of us at one point in our lives. Now, Momma didn't mind having an imagination, but she was one of the most grounded women in the universe. No big words for Momma she simply said, "You can dream you had a million dollars and wake up only to discover empty hands." Momma was quick to point out that the million dollars was indeed within reach, but we had to work for it and nothing in life came easy.

Being a single Mom of nine, the road was rocky, but that was cool because the common denominator that all us kids felt was love. Let's face it, motherhood is a profession in itself it takes serious skills to maneuver thru that tightrope.

Momma was like that ride or die chick. You would want this lady as your wing man.

Momma simply loved us one blood one love.

I have to be honest and tell ya that it wasn't till I was an adult that I saw my mother fix her own plate of food. The nine of us ate first and she always ate what was left. As a child you buy her reason of not being hungry or too tired to eat. As an adult the reality sinks in, my cubs eat first and if there is anything left then I eat. Damn I am still humbled by that to this day.

The currents that flow between a single black mother and her children are often deepened and intensified by life itself.

The bottom line is that Momma was a strong woman sometimes beaten, but never truly broken. She always wanted another world that would be better for us. Lord she was fierce in that determination. One year after her going home to be with the lord I can still feel it, its tangible it doesn't go away. Momma had a deep well of spiritual strength that was epic.

I don't know if Momma said one day at a time, but that's how it played out. And ya know what? That's been and is alright with me.

Everything that I have learned about love and sacrifice I learned from my Momma. Momma absorbed, accepted and gave, she was always giving. If she didn't have she was trying to figure out a way to get.

Something Momma said sticks with me to this day, "I'll be with you always girl, even when you don't want me to." Well at the time she said it, it was pretty freaking irritating. And now, I'm counting on it.

In the privileged world of today, it's so easy to forget our strong African women, our foremothers. Women like Momma who blazed the trails for us.

Momma was strong and powerful. She was the woman who cooked and cleaned for other families so we could eat and have clothes on our back. Momma literally worked from sun up to sun down all for us, always for us.

Momma refused to submit to the intoxication of poverty because she simply wanted to instill pride in all her children. As a result, we knew which fold to use at an elegant dinner, we knew it was an absolute no no to put our elbows on the table, and we knew to place the napkin gently on our lap. And Lord knows we better not walk on anyone's grass. With Momma it was these values that stuck.

My mother told each and every one of us this simple truth. "Nothing comes to a sleeper but a dream." Now I'm sure many mother's told her children this, but it was like momma had a patent on it. We all believed it.

We didn't have a soap opera view of life. Leave it to beaver was cool, but the bottom line is we grew up knowing life was what we made it.

My consciousness of the world beyond my family was simple. Momma said, "She put her panties on the same way you do." Momma stressed the point that those that had more than me were no better than me and I was no better than those that had less.

Momma said with each generation it will and has gotten better. "I done better than my momma and you girls will do better than me," had to respect her raw honesty.

Education was so serious for momma, old girl didn't play. She scraped and hustled to send us to Catholic schools because she thought that was a better education. Now momma only made through the sixth grade yet to me she was the most well-read woman I ever knew. Truth be told if we didn't share DNA, she still would have been a cool chick to me.

Momma always said if you can read you can do anything. I think I got my love of books from Momma. Though we lived from pay check to paycheck growing up, anything we wanted to pursue momma made it happen.

Momma always said, "Knowledge is power that one thing that no one can take away."

I feel I would not be an author had momma not told me I can do anything I want. Lord the woman made all her children feel 10 feet tall.

Momma was a strong believer in speaking proper English. I always wondered why. Her response, "Simple baby, English is a strategy in the overall battle of civil rights."

Momma was an advocate of education, though she could not provide financial support for us to go to college, by God her moral support was fierce.

"Use that head for more than a hat rest," Momma said, and she meant it.

Momma instilled within us a sense of identity. Stand up straight she would say. She knew what each of our hangs ups were and she sawed through them like a hot laser sword.

Growing up in K-Town in Chicago we were raised to be tough but lord knows we better not start any crap.

My brother Greg vividly recalls Momma saying, "If one comes home with blood all better come home with blood." One blood one love, it was that simple with Momma.

Momma had a potty mouth for sure, and her thoughts were simple and pure, "don't give a fuck about nobody who don't give a fuck about you." Oh yea, she told all of us that at a very early age. Yep, Hazel kept it real.

It's so funny, Momma passed on February 12, 2013 and that was the first time in years that all seven of us spent any time together. And the wonder of all wonders is we are all alphas. Go figure, right? How could we be anything else with hazel for Momma?

Momma always said, "being different isn't easy, but not being true to yourself is unacceptable." That stuck with all of us.

Momma always said, "You don't need no telling when you see Jesus for yourself."

"Get your own Ricky." She told my big brother. "Being in and out of relationships living with women, you are ultimately responsible for you. You can't expect anybody to take care of you; all you need is yo Momma and a dime," she said. That must have stuck with my bro because he got his own.

The fundamentals of life were pretty simple for Momma. She taught us the meaning of sacrifice. She taught us compassion. Even though we didn't have much, all of K-town knew Momma Hawkins had a plate of food or a warm place to stay if needed. She taught us the act of charity, always give God what was his and everything else would fall into place. She taught us to follow our heart, she really believed in that. Above all else, she taught us to do what was right. Each and every one of us remembers her telling us, "I don't like that Tracy." Insert anyone of her children's name here, it applied to us all.

I remember the moment I knew beyond a shadow of a doubt I could trust Momma. I was young and had done something. I can't remember what it was, but I know I had no business doing it. Momma said this to me. "I don't care if you killed a nigga, you come tell me and we will figure out where to bury the body."

Those were powerful words for a five year old child to grasp.

Well I never killed anyone, but from then on I knew I could trust Momma with anything. Momma wasn't a saint and as she taught all of us accept people for whom and what they were.

Momma offered advice if one was receptive. She was God-fearing, but we didn't go to church every Sunday, although she was a member of First Baptist forever. She loved to gamble and it didn't matter what she bet on, be it the horses, lottery, or card games; you name it she bet on it.

Momma had many good friends. I remember her telling me, "baby don't lie to yourself or your best friend, you will lose all reality." I still remember that to this day.

She told all us, "All closed eyes ain't sleep." Boy oh boy did that stick with us all.

When we didn't understand something she would say, "Chile just keeps on living. Ain't nothing new under the sun."

Momma was one of the most nonjudgmental people I knew, it was easy for Momma, she would say, "live and let live."

I had a tendency to be a serious child. I think that worried Momma on some level, she always told me "live is short, it's up to you to make it sweet." In all honesty I am still working on that.

"Whatever you do, be the best," Momma told us. "If you gonna be a ho, be a good ho. If you gonna be a street sweeper, be the very best street sweeper there is, take pride in self and nobody can ever tear you down."

Momma taught us to follow the voice inside and to trust our instincts. I remember she would always say, "Listen to the good angel, not the bad one, and baby if you listen carefully you will always be able to tell the difference."

One thing I can say, Momma was consistent. She still echoes in me and my siblings mind to be proud of who we are. She taught us to be proud of our family and stick together. She taught us about racism and black pride. Momma thought the more we knew about black pride, racism couldn't poison our minds.

The last few years of Momma's life we spent a lot of time together. She told me the story about a kid in her class that would get popped upside the head for dragging out the word pussy in pussy willow. I laughed and laughed; trust me you had to be there.

She also told me the story about her great great Grandmother being a slave. She said, "They probably never told you this in school, but over 100 years ago a 34 year school teacher changed the world."

I said, "who Momma Abraham Lincoln?"

She said, "Chile Lincoln was a lawyer."

She said, "No, this guy's name was Joshua." Well, I later did my research and found out she was talking about Joshua Lawrence Chamberlain, a Civil War hero.

Momma made stories sound so exciting, that was her gift.

She explained how everything and everybody somehow would touch everybody's life. She spoke about how the man was in the union army and his sole duty was to hold off the rebels in a town called Gettysburg, Pennsylvania. Eighty-thousand men were in front, Chamberlain and his men took up the rear. Their one and only goal was not to let the rebels cross the line.

She told about the man's total commitment to the task. She told about the first, second and third charge. Thousands of men died and the union ran out of ammo, but Chamberlain himself got shot and his belt buckle stopped the bullet. I tell you I was absolutely mesmerized by her storytelling.

She said at one point they had to get ammo from the dead, but the union kept fighting. "You see baby girl failure was not an option." Momma said.

She said with the fourth charge the rebels almost made it past the wall and the union was down to about eighty men. Momma said the only thing she could think of was Chamberlain had a deep seeded conviction, the inability to do nothing. By the fifth charge, it was either do or die, and sure enough Momma said they came back with reinforcement and crossed the line. By this time my heart was beating so fast, it felt like it was about jump out my chest. Even though I already knew the story, I was pretty surprised that Momma knew the story of Gettysburg. Though it was silly of me to be surprised, Momma lived for almost a century and that's a long time to forget.

Momma continued with her story, the union was getting slaughtered and down to eighty men. All they could see were more and more grey uniforms coming at them. She told how they had nothing but blood, guts, and an extreme desire of the inability to do nothing, she kept stressing that point.

By now I was so quiet; you could hear a fly piss on cotton.

Momma said Chamberlain stood on top of the hill and there were over four hundred men to his eighty. He yelled charge, charge, charge full speed ahead. The rebels were certain these were not the same men they had been faced with; surely they sent for reinforcement. Momma said that was not the case, just one man with the inability to do nothing. In less than several minutes Chamberlain had captured the confederate captain.

I asked Momma where she heard that story and why it was so important to her. Her response was classic Hazel, "I have forgotten more than you will ever remember baby girl, just keep on living'."

She pointed out that Chamberlain is still touching lives today. If it were not for him, the south would have won the war and we could all still be slaves.

She said, "Anytime you have a chance to make a difference do it."

She preceded this story with asking me what I knew about George Washington Carver. *Where was this going*, I thought. I told her that he created peanut butter. Hazel got down to schooling me. She said baby girl he flapped his wings much more than that. I asked what she meant by 'flapped his wings'.

She said, "girl, don't you know a butterfly can flap its wings and set molecules of air in motion which would move other molecules in the air callable of creating a mighty storm on the other side of the earth."

At this point, I am in total awe, my 89 year old Mother schooling me on the butterfly effect.

I asked her if she saw the movie and she looked at me like what movie, girl this life.

Momma inspired

I think we all learned from her never be afraid hold your head up high and fight all things head on. She had a way about her that you knew she wasn't afraid of anyone or anything and by God always stand, just stand.

Momma was a simple woman, "I can show a nigga better than I can tell 'em.'"

She was raw, she was truth, and she always kept it real.

You have heard the term 'it's a hard knock life', well Momma took the make lemonade out of lemons to a whole other level.

Momma taught us to face adversity with a clear mind and a strong vision. She believed what didn't kill you made you strong. Crying was ok for a moment, but only a moment.

"You can cry and feel sorry for yourself or you can wipe those tears and go on with your life." I thought that was harsh and to be honest, I still don't know how it felt when she first told me that. But I will tell you I dried my eyes and moved on with my life each time and the world did not fall off its axis.

Momma always believed our lives would be better than hers. When it came to her children Momma had a saying. "Every old crow thinks her chick is as white as snow, and you know a crow is black as hell."

Spirituality and faith

Momma had it in spades, she was a simple woman. I used to love to hear her say in reference to the bible, "And I believe every word that it says." She didn't try to push God on us, it just was. Her favorite thing to say was "If you see Jesus for yourselves you don't need no telling." That could apply to almost anything.

She said, "Don't ever begrudge anyone for what they have; the Lord knows how they got it, you just pray for what you want."

She would say, "Don't you know if he provides for the sparrow what he will do for you?"

She would always say, "Don't get so big for you britches don't you know your arms too short to box with God?"

She always said, "God is with you even when I'm not." I'm count on that to this day.

This is one of my favorites on spirituality.

We need to find God, and he cannot be found in noise and restlessness, God is the friend of silence, see how nature trees, flowers, grass-grows in silence; see the stars, the moon and the sun, how they move in silence... We need silence to be able to touch souls.

Mother Teresa

Work ethics

To Momma work ethics stared with schooling. Her philosophy was she wasn't going to be up at the school more than us. My brother Artilus recalls the time when he hid behind the refrigerator trying to play hooky from school. Of course Momma caught him, whipped his ass, and made him get dressed. She didn't even give him time to comb his hair. She promptly dragged him off to school. The moral of the story, don't mess with Momma when it comes to getting an education.

Momma felt the way you behaved in school would shape your work ethics. She was our role model, the poster child for good work ethics. She taught us to be honest and hardworking. Never play 'big I little u'. She told us to always be willing to extend a helping hand to others because if all had a little bit no one would be without nothing. Wow, little did we know by helping other's we would come to see how truly blessed we were despite the few material possessions we had.

Relationships

My sister Wanda recalls getting ready for a date in a very provocative outfit. Momma didn't mince words she told her leave something to the imagination Chile. Vintage Hazel, she always gave it straight up no chaser. She often said, "Don't get in them streets and let someone else raise you, that's my job." She reminded us that relationships were about concessions and compromise.

She often said, "if you gonna be a fool don't be a damned fool."

Momma was always on our side because we were her chicks, but she always taught us right from wrong. Momma was pretty clear on the golden rule; always treat people the way you want to be treated.

Ravinia Smith, my Brother Terry's girlfriend at the time recalled such a time vividly. Ravinia lived on the far south side of Chicago and we lived in K-Town. Chicago is famous for its harsh winters; Ravinia traveled all that distance to see Terry. Ravinia recalls Momma telling her to shake her head. Thinking her head still had snow on it, she did just that. Momma said, "Girl you come all this way to see Terry, cluck a cluck cluck all water and no brains." Momma told her. That was classic Hazel, and to this day Ravinia uses that line on her daughter when she is behaving foolish.

Momma reminded us that ultimately we are someone's role model, even when we think no one is watching, behave accordingly. She often said, "To thine own self be true and the rest will fall in place."

She wanted us to understand bread cast upon the waters will always come back to you a million fold, give out good and good comes back to you, give out evil and it's coming right back to you. Everything under the sun, if it goes round it will sho-nuf come back.

Momma was always a live and let live woman. She told each of us, "If you can lie down next to him you can sho-nuf stand up next to him." She often used the classic; every tub has to stand on its own bottom.

Now I don't know if she told this to my brothers, but my sister Yolanda lives by this rule and she been married for 20 years. "Don't lay down with a nigga with no purpose in mind cause all you gonna get is a wet ass and a rambling mind!"

To my brothers she said, "Well I guess if you feed the child long enough it will start to look like you!"

As for her own baby daddies, my brother Terry recalls these words, "that's your daddy love him if you can, 'cause I sho in the hell don't have to."

What can I say, Momma was sushi raw. She was never judgmental; remember every tub had to sit on its own bottom.

Family

Hazel was clear on that as my brother Tyrone recollects, "no matter what y'all stick together." Well it's seven of us living and we are still sticking together. Momma said it, that's all, that's enough; we are doing what she commanded of us.

My niece Rachel reflected on a visit with her grandmother. She recalls chatting about her friends and Momma told her you got only three real friends, me, your Momma and Jesus. Momma didn't apologize for her feelings, this is how she felt.

Humor

Momma comforted us with one simple line. "My mind don't lead me." Lord if we had a nickel for all the times she said that, we would sure enough be rich!!

Politics

Momma was one of the most learned women I have ever been blessed to meet. Despite Momma's dream of becoming a nurse, she only finished the sixth grade. She had a wide range of interest that trickled down to all her children. As early as the age six I remember my Mother adding the President of the United States to her prayers.

As a family we talked about why one should pray for the president. These are some of Momma's thoughts on that, "This is the country in which I was born. It doesn't matter how we vote or even who we vote for. Always pray God bless the president. Pray for his wisdom and health. Pray God bless him with good ideas and change his mind of the bad ones. Pray that God grants him with the spirit of discernment in our nations as well as our brother and sister nations."

Momma often said, "If you don't exercise your hard earned right to vote, then you're a damn fool." Guess it was a no brainer to Hazel.

War

"War is about power and land and that's been the way of it since the beginning of time." Momma didn't have to draw pictures; her words were very easy to understand.

Wisdom

"Don't be so busy denying your mistakes so that you can't learn from them, after all Chile that's why pencils have erasers." With those simple words one can build a foundation of life's lessons. Momma often said, "How you going to love someone else if you don't love yourself? I want you to have an understanding of people. You need to realize everyone is different, but the basic thing about people is understanding the different tones of emotions. Always be mindful of others' insecurities of their distress, and most of all their dreams, never try to quill a person's dreams." I carry that thought to this very day.

Regrets

Momma said, "Regrets are meaningless, live your life for you and no one else.

I wanted to share a bit about the things that resonated with my family and myself that our Mother said. How she made us feel. The very essence of a woman with a sixth grade education that raised nine children through strength, determination and will. Momma often said to accomplish anything it's 90% mental, and I truly believe that. In fact, I can say beyond a shadow that that's how our family live life.

As the Jewish proverb goes, 'God could not be everywhere and therefore he made Mothers'.

She was great because she could make something out of nothing. Great is an adjective that means marvelous, high in rank, noble, proud, accomplished, high minded everlasting and wealthy. Yea, that sums up Hazel Lee Garrett.

You see, despite the fact that she is no longer on earthy plane with us; we will always be eternally connected to her. In her womb, she cared for us nine months; she provided nourishment for our bodies. When we were born, it was her breast that we suckled on to grow stronger. As we grew older she molded us, shaped us, caressed us, loved us, read to us, sung to us, taught us and prayed for us.

For the record, I am not trying to paint the perfect picture of Motherhood. Before I leave you to what other Mothers have said, I want to share with you one more Hazel gem, "right wrong or indifferent, it is what it is."

Following is what some of what others' Mommas have said...

"Love is the only thing we have that never runs out, cause if the cup is have full simply fill it back up."

Estella Jackson

Mother of Samantha Smith

"It ain't going to be no ass kicking it's going to be a fight!"

Shirley Banks

Mother of Robert Banks

"Life goes on my time here is over, now it's time to take care of you and your son."

Isabella Warren

Mother of Swanee Warren

"Just keep on living."

Brenda Aytch

Mother Lottie Aytch

"Everybody won't tell the same lie on you."

Rena Mae Wilson

Mother of Linda Wilson

"Girl don't fool with him. It's something about him; I just ain't figured it out yet."

Ms. Deb Patterson

Mother Geraldine Patterson

"Always treat a woman the way you would treat me."

Claudia Steward

Mother of Vincent Steward

"You can go crazy, but don't act no damn fool."

Florence Pryor

Mother of Monique Pryor

"Never call a woman a bitch and always respect women like queens."

Patricia Rivers

Mother of Shawn Rivers

"Don't make anything you can't take care of."

Louise Barnes Chandler

Mother of Stacy Barnes

"You don't have to keep bragging about having good taste. If you have it, it will show."

Maryann Williams

Mother of Dana Williams

"If you going to be in front of someone. Don't be out front and make an ass of yourself."

Clara Smart

Mother of Charles Smart

"If you only have two pair of pants, wash one and wear one. You will always have clean clothes."

Manlia Cutts

Mother of Joseph Cutts

"Know that your actions cannot be hoarded saved for later or used selectively because that would be a shame."

Melissa Jones

Mother of Terry Jones

"Live your life to the fullest son, not through others, but go out there and grab a piece of life for yourself."

Sara Meyers

Mother of Kevin Meyers

"A woman is not fully dressed without her bling; it sets the tone be it serene or sassy!"

Sissy Alers

Mother of Clara Alers

"All that glitters ain't gold."

Ola Green

Mother of Jackie Green

"Knowledge is and always will be the prime need of the hour, Son never forget that."

Celine Dodds

Mother of Carlos Harris

"Allen you are smart and you can think for yourself, you have been given opportunities that I only dreamed about. Don't take that for granted and always be willing to share your success with others less fortunate than you."

Sabrina Keys

Mother of Allen Keys

"Don't talk with your mouth full... Boy answer me!!

Ola Mae Wilson

Mother of Donnie Nelson

Venus' Mother told her this about getting into trouble, "Keep on living you just mad cause your ass in the grass."

Derrick Williams' Mother told him this about taking hard knocks, "Weeping may endure for the night..."

Terza Eliaz Solomon's Mother told her this feminist bit of humor. "I became a feminist at 14 years old. In 1926 before even knowing what that word meant, after hearing gossip at a wedding concerning the bride's virginity. I thought to myself, does the groom also matter, after all that is probably how the bird lost hers."

Captola Wade remembers this from a mentor, "Though 1000 people will say you can't, you just need one reason why you can."

Portia Dowd remembers this from her youth. "Always do the best that you can."

Susan Johnson's Mother Lola told her this about self-reliance, "Every tub must sit on its own bottom."

Isabella Clifton's Mom told her this bit of wisdom, "enough is enough and too much is just foolish.

Stella Williams remembers her mom saying, "I thought I could change the world. It took me a life time to figure out I can't change the world, I can only change myself. And honey child let me tell you, that ain't easy!"

Eva Thompson's Mother told her, "People won't remember what you say; they will remember what you do. So be smart, smart enough to be a lady."

"Let the food stop your mouth," is what Lena Evans told her daughter Cassie Lockhart. Cassie explained that her Mother meant shut up and listen.

Minnie Holman's Mother told her, "Prepare for war in time of peace." She explained her Mother meant hope for the best, but never be shocked or surprised by the worst.

Rochelle Stevenson's Mother told her this about living life to the fullest, "Whatever makes you happy do it! If you see something you want buy it! Don't depend on a man for anything. Life is short, enjoy and live it 'til God says it's over."

Shauna Gibbs Mother told her this about motherhood, "Your job as a Mother is to protect your child, she is buried in Africa and Africa is buried in her. Embrace your motherhood for Mothers are superior beings, that's why they reign supreme."

Debbie Rivers' Mother Ann Money told her, "Education remains the key to success, but that's only 10%, the other 90% is up to you."

Yolanda Owens Mother Hazel Garret Mother told her this about inner beauty. You are a pretty black girl and you can walk slowly through a crowd."

Halle Stone's Mother shared with her, "you got to forgive otherwise they will just take free rent in your head."

There are generations of unborn Mothers whose very lives will be shifted and shaped by the moves they make and the actions they take for tomorrow and the next day. Yes everything we do really does matter. Through God and our Mothers we have been created as one of kind on this great blue marble and there has never been anyone like us and there will never be. Our spirit, thoughts and feelings; our ability to reason and act all exist in no one else. The rarities that make us special are no mere accident or quirk of fate; it started with a Mother's decision to bring us in the world, much like the decision of the Mother over 2000 years ago.

Thank you all for sharing your Mothers' Mother wit, the wisdom and humor of Mothers is timeless

Authors Note

Thank you everyone for sharing the words of wisdom or advice your Mothers shared with you to motivate, inspire, or simply help you realize your dreams. If you would like to share your Mothers' words of wisdom for future editions of this book, please send them to Tracy Hawkins at authorthawk2222@gmail.com

BIO...

Tracy Hawkins Bio....

Born and raised on the west side of Chicago, affectionately called K-Town. Tracy never saw a book she didn't want to read. From the poetry of Langton Hughes to the rhymes of Dr. Seuss, books became her passion. Something happened with all that reading, the zeal to write!! If Tracy is not writing she is thinking about writing.

Tracy majored in journalism with a minor in psychology. She resides in a suburb of Chicago IL. Where she is currently working on several literary projects.

www.ingramcontent.com/pod-product-compliance
Lightning Source LLC
Chambersburg PA
CBHW061506170626
46811CB00004B/1618